The Three Little KITTENS

illustrated by

MILO WINTER

LAUGHING ELEPHANT   MMXIII

The three little kittens,
They lost their mittens,
And they began to cry,
"Oh! mother dear,
We greatly fear,
That we have lost
our mittens!"

"What! lost your mittens,
You naughty kittens,
Then you shall
    have no pie,"
"Mee-ow--mee-ow--mee-ow,
Then we shall have no pie."

The three little kittens,
They found their
mittens, And they
began to cry,

"Oh! mother dear,
See here, see here,
See, we have found our
mittens!"

"Put on your
mittens,
You silly kittens
And you may have
some pie."

"Purr-rr--

purr-rr--

purr--rr,

Oh, let us have some pie."

The three little kittens,
Put on their mittens,
And soon ate up
the pie;

"Oh! mother dear,
We greatly fear
That we have soiled
        our mittens."

"What! soiled your
mittens,
You naughty kittens!"
Then they began to sigh,

"Mee-ow--

mee-ow--

mee-ow,"

Then they began to sigh,

The three little kittens

They washed their mittens

And hung them up
to dry;

"Oh! mother dear,
Do you not hear,
That we have washed
   our mittens?"

"What!
washed your
mittens,
You good little kittens!

Hush, I smell a rat
   close by!
Hush! hush!"
"Mee-ow--mee-ow,
We smell a rat close by."

Laughing
ELEPHANT

ISBN/EAN: 9781595833747

THIS PRODUCT CONFORMS TO CPSIA 2008

THIRD PRINTING · PRINTED IN CHINA THROUGH COLORCRAFT LTD., HONG KONG · ALL RIGHTS RESERVED
THIS IS A REPRINT OF A BOOK FIRST PUBLISHED BY THE MERRILL PUBLISHING COMPANY C.1938

LAUGHING ELEPHANT
3645 INTERLAKE AVENUE NORTH **SEATTLE, WA** 98103

LAUGHINGELEPHANT.COM